One Rainy Day

by Donna Taylor

Illustrated by Ken Edwards

Based on the books by • Norman Bridwell •

SCHOLASTIC INC.
New York   Toronto   London   Auckland   Sydney
Mexico City   New Delhi   Hong Kong   Buenos Aires

Clifford wants to play.

But . . .

Pitter-patter!
Pitter-patter!

Rain!

Clifford cannot play.

What a pain!

Emily Elizabeth comes
to read Clifford a story.

"This story is about a girl named Gail," Emily Elizabeth says. "Her mother and father gave her a boat.

It is a nice day.

Gail wants to sail the boat.

Away she goes!

Oh, no! Gail is lost
at sea!

Which way is home?

Who can help her?

Around and around
goes the boat.

Then . . . hooray!
Here comes a big
red dog!

He saves the day!

Gail is okay!

She hugs him and he
wags his tail.

And that's the way the story ends," says Emily Elizabeth.

Clifford gives her a big kiss!

This is a fun way to spend . . .

. . . a rainy day!